THORFINN THE NICEST VIKING

For Isla Rose – D.M.

To Summer the Viking warrior princess – R.M.

Young Kelpies is an imprint of Floris Books
First published in 2015 by Floris Books
Second printing 2016

The publisher acknowledges subsidy from
Creative Scotland towards the publication
of this volume

MIX
Paper from
responsible sources
FSC® C117931
www.fsc.org

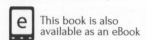

This book is also
available as an eBook

FIFE COUNCIL	
123456	
PETERS	05-Apr-2016
JF	£5.99
JFHUM	LO

British Library CIP data available
ISBN 978-178250-158-9
Printed & Bound by MBM Print SCS Ltd, Glasgow

Thorfinn
and the
Awful Invasion

written by David Macphail
illustrated by Richard Morgan

Young Kelpies

OSWALD
WISE MAN OF INDGAR

VELDA

RAGNAR
THE GRANNY-WRESTLER

PERCY
THE PIGEON

INDGAR VILLAGE

COW SHEDS

CHAPTER 1

Harald the Skull-Splitter was a Viking chief. Like all Vikings, he'd been given a tough name when he came of age. Skull-Splitter was the roughest and toughest name his parents could think of. And Harald was one of the roughest and toughest Vikings EVER.

One day, Harald came back from a sea voyage. He kicked open his front door in the usual Viking way.

BLAM!

"I'm hungry! What's for dinner?"

Then he let out a cry of horror, for standing in
the kitchen was the most terrifying thing he had
ever seen. More terrifying than the two-headed sea
monster of Kroll. More terrifying than the painted
cannibals of Caledonia.

It was his son, Thorfinn.

And he was doing the dishes!

"Great Thor! What on earth do you think you are doing?" Harald shouted. His great bushy beard glimmered gold in the light from the fire.

Thorfinn turned round, a kindly smile spreading across his face.

"Greetings, dear Father!" he said. "How pleased I am to see you. Did you have a pleasant voyage?"

Harald screwed up his face in disgust.

"Pleased? Pleasant voyage? Bah! I'm a Viking, by Odin! I burn! I pillage! I bite chickens' heads off and spit them at old ladies! I do not have pleasant voyages. Do you understand?"

"Oh yes," said Thorfinn. "Sorry, I forgot."

Harald's face screwed up even more.

"Mother was so tired," said Thorfinn. "She

dragged a whole goat up from the bottom of the fjord. I thought she could do with a nap, so I sent her off to bed with a nice cup of tea, while I did the dishes."

"A... A... A nap!"

Thorfinn's father was spitting with rage now, and his eye was twitching. Harald had an incredibly twitchy eye – probably from all those battles he'd fought in. He'd been in about two hundred battles. He was fearless.

"Viking wives don't have naps. Viking women are strong! They can chop down trees! They terrify wild bulls!" Harald looked again at his son and groaned.

"And Viking sons don't make nice cups of tea, do you hear?"

"But Dad, it's hard work looking after Viking families," Thorfinn replied. "I mean, all that eating meat with bare hands and beer splashing all over the place. No wonder the poor woman is tired."

Harald saw the kindness and gentleness in his son's eyes, and all of a sudden his anger melted away. How could anyone be angry with Thorfinn? Even Harald, a man who was known as 'The Terror of the North Sea', couldn't be angry with him. He sighed and sat down, then picked Thorfinn up and plonked him on his knee.

"What am I going to do with you?" he said. "You go around the village taking your helmet off to people and saying 'Good day'. You make jam, you drink tea, you help old people across the street. It's not on. I mean, you don't have any decent Viking qualities at all."

Harald often wondered if his son had been swapped at birth, perhaps by a witch. Or maybe one of the Viking gods did it for a laugh. Maybe his real son was being brought up by a quiet family in one of those awful peaceful countries where no one had battles.

"Hmm..." Harald said under his breath. "What will I do with you? What, what, what?"

CHAPTER 2

Thorfinn was at a very important age. Soon he would have to earn his Viking name. Thorfinn had three brothers: Wilfred the Spleen-Mincer, Sven the Head-Crusher and Hagar the Brain-Eater. But what sort of a name was Thorfinn going to get?

"I dread to think what we'll call you," Harald said. "Thorfinn the Neat-and-Tidy, perhaps. Thorfinn the Jam-Maker?"

A huge shiver ran right up Harald's back, and Thorfinn gave a worried look.

"Dearest Father, have you caught a chill? Would

you like me to fetch you a pair of slippers or a quilted blanket?"

"Quilted blanket indeed!" Harald sighed and slapped his own forehead. "Can you guess what my enemies would say if they found me wrapped up in a quilted blanket?"

"I expect they'd say, 'Oooh, I want one of them,'" replied Thorfinn. "After all, it does get very cold in Norway."

"Oh dear, oh dear, this is a terrible situation for a Viking chief's son," said Harald. "People are beginning to talk. I'm going to have to do something drastic. Yes, I will make a Viking of you somehow."

"Well that would make me very happy too, Father. I want to make you proud of me," said Thorfinn.

"I need to go outside for a think," said Harald.

Whenever Harald had to think, he practised throwing axes at the trees. It made his brain work, he said. When Thorfinn's father went outside to think, everybody in the neighbourhood ran indoors and hid. He had a terrible aim. Thorfinn thought this was probably due to the twitchy eye.

After a few minutes of axe throwing, during which he hit three eagles, a moose and a whale basking in the fjord, Harald came bursting back through the door.

BLAM!

A mighty laugh bellowed from inside his great barrel-shaped chest.

"Bah! I have it, young Thorfinn!" he cried. "I have it. You are going to make a name for yourself, by Thor! I am leaving on a voyage of destruction in two days, and you, my son, are coming with me!"

This idea sounded brilliant to Thorfinn. He'd never been abroad. In fact, he'd never been outside his own fjord.

"How exciting! I've always wanted to go on a cruise."

He jumped into his father's arms, and Harald whirled him around and set him down again. Like most Vikings, Harald was fiery and excitable, and he

21

often got a bit carried away. He pulled his hammer out of his breeches, clutched it in both hands and brought it down with a mighty clobber on the dining table. The table split in two –

CRACK

– and a big bowl of jam catapulted up into the air.

"Watch out!" cried Thorfinn, but it was too late.

The bowl spun around and came hurtling down on to his father's head. Jam splurted all over his beard and across his chest.

"Blaaah!" cried Harald, his booming voice echoing inside the bowl.

"Oh dear, that's another table ruined," said Thorfinn, thinking of the twelve other tables his

father had smashed up in the last year. Fortunately,

Thorfinn was a dab hand at DIY too.

"Mmmm, good jam, though!" said Harald.

CHAPTER 3

The next day, in the market, all the Viking boys were boasting about how tough their families were.

"My grandfather was Sigmund the Sword-Slasher," said one boy proudly. "His sword was a metre long and he could split trees in half with a single blow!"

The biggest of the boys was called Olaf. He had a huge bulgy red nose and a chin like a jagged cliff. He barged his way to the front, munching on a pile of nuts.

"Ha! That's nothing!" he chomped. "My great-grandfather was called Hagar the Throat-Throttler, and he was so strong he once wrestled a moose. When he got bored wrestling the moose, he went and wrestled a bear instead."

The younger boys all gasped in admiration.

Velda, one of the Viking girls, came running up, swinging an axe. Everyone leapt out of the way. "My father was a great warrior too, you know!" she cried.

Velda's father was called Gunga the Navigator. Unfortunately, rumour had it that he was actually a bit rubbish at navigating. He'd got lost on one of his voyages and hadn't been seen since. Velda had sworn she would find him one day. But a girl would never be allowed on a longship. The Vikings thought it was unlucky.

"Girls can't come on voyages," said Olaf, and the other boys shouted their agreement.

"Why not? I can fight better than any of you." She could too. Velda had proven it many times. That was how Olaf got his bulgy nose.

"You're a girl!" Olaf cried. "Now buzz off!"

Velda stomped away, dragging her axe behind her. Only Thorfinn gave her a sympathetic smile. He was sitting at the edge of the market, feeding his pet pigeon, Percy.

Percy was a lovely white colour with grey freckles. Thorfinn was the only person in the village to own a pigeon, and Percy was special because he was a homing pigeon. He would often carry messages and news to people in other fjords, but

he always came home to Thorfinn. Thorfinn found out what was happening outside the fjord before anyone else did.

The other boys laughed when they saw Thorfinn with Percy.

"Look, there's Thorfinn. I heard he's getting to go on a voyage. Can you believe it?" said one of them. None of the other boys had been on a voyage yet.

They were all jealous.

"This just isn't fair," said Olaf. "Why should he get to make a name for himself? He's no Viking. Not like us."

The boys all agreed that Thorfinn was a rubbish Viking. They started joking about him.

"What name will he come back with? Thorfinn the Milk-Drinker? Thorfinn the Shelf-Fixer? Thorfinn the Napkin-Folder? Ha ha ha!"

Then they made up a song. The Vikings loved singing rowdy songs.

"Oh-oh-oh-oh, Thorfinn will a-raiding go,
Ay-ay-ay-ay, without delay he'll run away..."

Thorfinn didn't mind. In fact, he was impressed that they'd made the words rhyme for once. He even joined in at one point.

Unfortunately, he was about to make a new name for himself.

Nuts were one of Percy the pigeon's favourite foods. As soon as Percy caught sight of the nuts in Olaf's hand he took to the air and started dive-bombing Olaf, trying to get at the nuts. Olaf tried to shoo him away, but Percy wanted those nuts, and no amount of shooing was going to put him off. Olaf stumbled backwards, then tripped over a barrel before splatting right into a big pile of horse dung. The nuts scattered everywhere, and Percy flew down and pecked them all up.

There was a stunned silence from the other boys. Olaf's dad was Erik the Ear-Masher, who was a rival to Thorfinn's dad as village chief. The Ear-Mashers

were a powerful family. You didn't want to make an enemy of Erik the Ear-Masher's son.

Olaf got up. He was covered in horse dung, and he glared at Thorfinn.

"How about this for a name," he snarled. "Thorfinn the Dunked-In-The Fjord."

"Oh dear," replied Thorfinn. "I'm awfully embarrassed by my pigeon's lack of manners. I should have said that he's mad about nuts."

"And there's no one more nuts than Olaf," said Velda, who had wandered back over to see what the fuss was about.

It was no use trying to reason with someone like Olaf. He charged at Thorfinn, roaring like a tiger.

But Thorfinn was nimble for a Viking, and Olaf

was big and clumsy. Thorfinn darted out of the way just in time, and Olaf leapt straight past him. He stumbled over a bucket, then landed with a

SPLODGE

in another, even bigger, pile of horse dung.

This one had bits of hay mixed in with it, which stuck to Olaf's hair and face. Thorfinn calmly knelt down and picked up his pigeon.

"Percy, you really are a naughty bird," he said.

Velda bellowed with laughter. "Clever Percy," she said. "And clever Thorfinn."

Olaf stood up, looking like a scarecrow with an attitude problem. He smelled terrible. All the boys in the market held their noses.

"EEUUUGH!"

Thorfinn left the market, still scolding Percy for his bad behaviour. Olaf swore that he would get his revenge. So did his whole family when they found out. Vikings are like that. They hold grudges.

CHAPTER 4

The day before Thorfinn's great voyage was due to begin, Percy arrived with a message tied to his leg. The message was from Oswald, the wise man of the village. It said:

COME AND SEE ME IMMEDIATELY, YOU YOUNG FOOL!

Oswald was Thorfinn's best friend in the world. He had a beard that stretched right down to his belly, and he was about eighty years old. He also had an incredibly loud, whiny voice, and he liked nothing more than to shout insults at people. He knew he could get away with it, because he was old.

Oswald had taught Thorfinn everything he knew. He'd taught him to read and write. He'd taught him mathematics and astronomy and navigation. He'd taught him how to speak languages. But what Thorfinn liked most about Oswald was his fantastic storytelling.

Night after night, groups of Vikings would huddle round the fire in the great hall where they had their meetings and feasts, and listen to the old wise man Oswald telling ancient Viking legends.

As soon as Thorfinn received Oswald's message, he set off to see him, whistling happily to himself as he walked through the forest and up the hill.

Oswald lived in a hut in the woods above a waterfall. Thorfinn climbed up and found him tending his garden outside. The old man greeted the boy with a whinny.

"I hear you are coming on our voyage, young

Thorfinn," he said. "Well, I can safely say that you have lost your head!"

"But what do you mean, old friend?" replied Thorfinn.

Oswald took him inside and sat him down beside the hearth. He'd made pancakes especially for Thorfinn's visit.

"Thorfinn, if anyone has the knowledge and the bravery to be a good Viking, it is you," said the old man. "Unfortunately, the ruthless bit is missing."

"I can't help being polite," said Thorfinn. "It's just the way I am."

Oswald got out a jar of Thorfinn's favourite jam, made from arctic berries. Together they ate the pancakes. To top it all off they shared pinecone tea, which Thorfinn drank with his pinkie raised in the air.

"Yummy," said Thorfinn, dabbing the edges of his mouth politely with a cloth.

"Voyages are very important to Vikings," said Oswald, leaning forward. As he did so, his long beard dipped into the pot of jam. "When a Viking goes on his first voyage, he comes of age. He performs heroic feats, brave deeds. That's how legends come about. It is every Viking's aim to have legends told about them after they are gone."

It was difficult talking to a man whose beard was dangling in a pot of jam. Thorfinn didn't want to embarrass his friend. He tried several times to

lift the beard and move the jam away without the
old man noticing, but Oswald kept moving it back.

"Oi! I'm not finished with that," Oswald said.

"Do you think they'll tell stories about me one day?" Thorfinn asked.

Oswald laughed. It sounded like a horse having a sneezing fit, and left Thorfinn covered in partly chewed pancake and jam.

"Perhaps," the old man said, composing himself. "Though maybe not the kind of legend you're thinking of. You see, my dear Thorfinn, you are unlike any Viking who has ever lived. The other Vikings do not understand you. They even laugh at you. But, if you remain true to yourself no matter what, then one day – just maybe – they will understand. And then, who knows, perhaps they will be telling stories about your adventures."

Oswald stood up. "Now where's that other pancake of mine gone?"

As he turned round Thorfinn spotted it. It was stuck to Oswald's bottom.

CHAPTER 5

That night, in the great hall, the Viking warriors held
a farewell feast. A long table stretched right up
the middle of the hall, and it was covered in huge
mounds of food.

There was roast chicken, boiled goat, grilled
reindeer, stewed hare, leg of moose, rack of lamb,
wild boar, fried squid, whole stuffed pig's head,
roasted pheasant, partridge soup...

And that was just the first course.

The Vikings liked to wash their food down

with lots and lots of ale, which they

drank from reindeer horns.

Thorfinn sat next to his father at the top of the table. Oswald sat opposite Thorfinn. At the far end of the table, Olaf's father, Erik the Ear-Masher, glowered at everyone. He only had one eye, of course. The other was covered by a patch. But there was enough glower in it for two.

Viking feasts were a messy business. They ripped the meat apart with their bare hands.

CRACK! CRUNCH! PING! RIP!

Then they all went silent and the room was filled with the sound of ravenous men eating.

CHOMP! GRIND! GNASH! CHEW! SLURP!

Then they spat the bones onto the floor for their dogs.

SNARL! GNAW! WOOF! SNAP!

Then there was the burping, the cheering, the farting, more cheering and the odd fight. For the Vikings, any banquet without at least three punch-ups was boring.

There was a glint in Chief Harald's eye as he picked up a huge roast leg of goat. He bit into it and a big squirt of grease shot out and hit him in the eye.

"Ouch!" he cried.

Thorfinn could only laugh. Unlike the others, he

was calmly cutting all his food up with a knife, and eating it in small pieces.

"You see, Father, if you take the time to chop your food, it's easier to eat," he said. But his father wasn't listening. He was too busy getting stuck into the goat's leg, a great sliver of meat hanging off his beard.

After drinking ale, the Vikings sang lots of songs. Then Thorfinn's father got up onto the table and blew a huge horn, which brought silence to the whole hall.

"Tomorrow morning at first tide we leave on another great voyage!" he cried. All the Vikings cheered.

"HUZZAH!"

"Our plan is to sail across the great North Sea to the land of the Scots."

To Thorfinn this was really exciting. After all, he'd never been to Scotland. He held up his hand.

"Pardon me, dearest Father." All eyes turned to look at Thorfinn. Harald felt scared for the first time in his life. Battles and fistfights didn't trouble him one bit, but his son embarrassing him? That was frightening.

"What shall we do when we get there?" Thorfinn asked. His father looked down at him as if he were mad.

"We all sit down and have a cup of tea, boy. What do you think?"

The other Vikings burst out laughing, slapping their thighs, but Thorfinn didn't get the joke. His eyes lit up.

"Is that really what we're going to do?"

"Don't be daft. We raid all the villages," said one Viking.

"We burn them to the ground," said another.

"We nick the gold from their churches," said a third.

To Thorfinn it seemed crazy to travel all that way just to burn everything. He thought it would be more fun to go sightseeing.

"I have heard that there's some wonderful scenery along the Scottish coast. Wouldn't it be great if we all took paints and brushes? We could sit on the deck and paint pictures. We could even have a competition."

Suddenly, the great hall fell deadly quiet. The Vikings all stared at each other, completely stunned. Thorfinn's father looked as if he'd just been asked to eat a salad.

"Bah! The idea! Can you imagine my ferocious Viking warriors flouncing around deck wafting paintbrushes? Are you mad?"

There was a huge burst of laughter, and then Olaf, Erik's son, stood up. He was still determined to get revenge on Thorfinn for the dung-heap incident.

"Listen to this one," he said, "Thorfinn the Sightseer!" The table erupted again.

Now Erik the Ear-Masher stood up. He drew his sword and whammed it down on the table, cutting the head off one of the roast pheasants and catapulting it into the air, along with a horn of ale. The pheasant head plopped into someone's beer. The man just shrugged and went on drinking. The horn spun round a couple of times before landing upside down on a dog's head. The dog yelped and then bolted out of the door. All eyes turned to Erik.

"Harald the Skull-Splitter," Erik said, "we do not want that son of yours on our voyage."

There was a big gasp from the other Vikings. Erik was challenging the chief of the village himself. It could only mean one thing.

There was going to be a fight!

CHAPTER 6

Harald's eye twitched dangerously. It would have been enough to send shivers up any man's spine – even Erik the Ear-Masher.

"Bah! Put that sword away, you one-eyed scoundrel!" said Thorfinn's father. "You dare challenge me? My son *will* be going. He *will* make a name for himself, by Odin! He *will* be a hero, and legends *will* be told about him for years to come."

Erik roared with laughter.

"You cannot be serious. This boy, the stuff of legends? My own son, Olaf, is a full year older than yours, and he is the strongest and fittest of all the boys, and yet he has never been on a voyage. This just isn't fair!"

Harald's temper was about to snap. His knuckles were gripping his sword and getting whiter by the moment, and his teeth were grinding like two giant millstones. The other Vikings looked from their chief to Erik and back again. They were waiting, even hoping, for a great fight to kick off.

Suddenly, Oswald, the wise man, stood up.

"If I may, Chief Harald?" he said. "I have a solution to the problem."

"What is your solution?" Harald replied, while still glaring at Erik the Ear-Masher.

"Why don't we take Erik's son too?" Oswald continued. "It might be good for young Thorfinn to have company."

"Hmm..." said Thorfinn's father, thinking. The stand-off continued. After a moment of further eye-twitching, he agreed.

"Very well, it is to be. Olaf, son of Erik the Ear-Masher, will come with us too. But let this be known ... if it were not for the boys, and for the fact that I'm in a very good mood, I would have lopped your head off, Ear-Masher!"

Slowly, Erik put away his sword. Harald's eye kept twitching until Erik sat down. The other Vikings cheered, and went back to guzzling their food, swallowing their ale and burping loudly.

Thorfinn nudged his father.

"Father, I am sorry to be such a bother. I do appreciate you taking me, you know. I'll try my best to be good."

Thorfinn's father roared, and bit the head off a stewed hare.

"I don't want you to be good, I want you to be *bad*! Understand?"

"You are *sooo* lucky, Thorfinn," said Velda after the feast. "I wish they would let me go with you." Thorfinn wished she was going too. She was brave and clever, everything a good Viking should be.

"When I am the chief I will let you go on voyages, I promise," he said.

Velda's face broke into a smile.

"I know you will," she said. And she went off swinging her axe happily.

Thorfinn went straight home. As he drifted off to sleep, Oswald's tales of ancient legends and heroes ran through his head. *Perhaps one day*, he thought, *people will sit round fires and tell stories about me.*

CHAPTER 7

Dawn broke upon the fjord. The sun was shining

brightly and the water was calm and peaceful.

Thorfinn packed everything he could

think of, including an extra-large

jar of jam and a pouch of

pinecones for making tea.

He couldn't go without

Percy, so he put his

pigeon in a cage

and took him

along.

When he got to the longship, most of the other Vikings were already there. They stood on the deck with their giant oars held aloft.

A warrior gave Oswald a piggyback on board, as he was too old to jump. Oswald hit the warrior with his stick and cursed him for nearly falling into the water.

"Watch it, you wretched piece of reindeer dung!"

Erik arrived, glaring at everyone with his one eye. Olaf brought along his hawk, a dark grey bird whose head was covered in a hood. Olaf stroked the bird's head as he taunted Thorfinn.

"Bet you're scared," Olaf said, and he barged past him.

Thorfinn didn't get angry. He just smiled back politely. He wasn't remotely scared. He was excited.

For the first time he was going out of the fjord to see the world.

Thorfinn's father barked orders from the back of the ship.

"Cast off, you pigs!"

The Vikings pushed the boat away from the pier with their oars. Thorfinn waved goodbye to his mother and the rest of the village. The longship turned round and they set off, singing rowdy songs all the way up the fjord towards the sea.

It wasn't long before the steep slopes of the mountains on either side opened out to a bright blue expanse of water. Harald ordered the men to hoist the sail. The boat caught the wind and they headed west.

Thorfinn could hardly believe his eyes. He had never seen anything so beautiful or so flat as the North Sea before. He went up to the front of the ship to watch the breakers crash off the prow. Behind him, the coast of his homeland disappeared out of sight.

"Next stop, Scotland!" cried his father.

"HUZZAH!" cried everyone.

Thorfinn remained at the front of the ship well into the afternoon. He was too excited to tear himself away. But he couldn't help wondering where Scotland was. Puzzled, he asked Oswald. The old wise man laughed.

"Ha! You young fool! We've a long way to go yet. Scotland is still far over the horizon."

Thorfinn stroked his chin. He liked to do that when he was thinking. It was a habit he'd picked up from Oswald himself, who stroked his beard nearly all the time.

"Wait a minute," Thorfinn said. "If the earth really is flat, like all Vikings say, then surely I should be able to see Scotland."

"Good thinking," said Oswald. "You are a man of learning. What shape do you think the world is, then?"

"Well, if Scotland is over the horizon, I would say that the earth is not flat at all, but curved. And, if I can't see Denmark, which is south, or Iceland, which is north, then I guess the world must be round, not flat."

Erik the Ear-Masher and his son overheard this comment, and both of them burst out laughing.

"Ha! Did you hear this nitwit?" said Erik. "He says the world isn't flat at all. He says it's round!"

The other Vikings laughed and slapped their thighs. "The world is round, like a pudding! The world *is* a pudding!"

"Somebody hold on to me," said Olaf. "I'm going to fall off the ship from laughing!"

Nearly every man on the ship was rocking back and forth and rolling around, laughing hysterically.

"Round, indeed!" laughed Erik.

Thorfinn looked at them all, smiling kindly. Only Oswald and his father failed to join in.

Harald's eye was twitching again. But now it was twitching at his own son. In fact both eyes were twitching. Harald had to wallop himself on the head to stop the other one. Then he gave a deep sigh, like an injured wild boar, and looked away.

When the laughter died down, Oswald took Thorfinn by the arm and spoke to him quietly.

"I'll tell you something, young Thorfinn," he said. "We men of learning have been trying to tell these idiots for years that the world is not flat. They won't believe us."

As the sun started to sink into the horizon, Thorfinn caught sight of another ship. It was sailing in the other direction, towards the east.

CHAPTER 8

"Excuse me, dear Father," Thorfinn said. "Would you please be so good as to look over there?"

Thorfinn pointed the ship out to him, but his father struggled to see in the glare of the sinking sun. The twitchy eye didn't help, of course. Thorfinn recognised the shape as a longship.

"They are Vikings too," said Thorfinn.

"You have the eye of an eagle, my son," said his father. "You might be of use to us yet."

Thorfinn's father alerted the rest of the men, and they all gathered round the front of the ship to see who it was. There was a great deal of excitement.

"They might be rivals of ours," said Thorfinn's father. "If they are, we will have to do battle with them. Or they might be friendly, in which case they can tell us where to find the best loot."

As the ship came closer, Erik the Ear-Masher spied a face he knew and declared that the ship was indeed friendly. This was met with a cheer. Vikings didn't like fighting other Vikings, you see. There was no loot to be had in it, and, besides, it wasn't half as much fun as fighting the Scots.

"By Thor!" exclaimed Erik. "It's the greatest Viking in Norway!"

"The greatest?" said Olaf. "Not ... not Ragnar the Granny-Wrestler!"

"It is," said Thorfinn's father. "By Valhalla itself, it is. It is! Ragnar the Granny-Wrestler!"

The whole crew grew very excited, whooping and cheering and waving their oars. Some of them even started belching the Viking national anthem, which they usually did only on special occasions, like holidays, royal weddings or village burnings.

This man must be important, Thorfinn thought.

"Excuse me, dear Oswald," he said, "but what do you know of this Ragnar fellow?"

"Ragnar the Granny-Wrestler is the toughest, most famous Viking in all the world. Legends are told about his feats all over Norway. The Queen Mother is one of his fans. Even the King asks for his autograph."

"I see," said Thorfinn. "How interesting."

"We shall invite him over to our ship!" announced Thorfinn's father.

"Yes," agreed Erik. "We must impress him."

"Ha! We will treat our very special guest like a prince," said Harald. He turned to the rest of the crew.

"Treat him like a guest should be treated, understand?"

Thorfinn nodded obediently and went over to the fire to put the kettle on.

The two crews exchanged a wave, and Ragnar's longship drew closer. A rope was thrown across the divide between them.

A giant man appeared at the other end of the rope. He started hauling himself across the gap with his hands, roaring and singing all the way.

"Oh-oh-oh-oh, a-pillaging villaging we will go,
Ay-ay-ay-ay, a-pillaging villaging every day."

A gigantic horn of ale hung round Ragnar's neck, and he stopped every once in a while to take a giant slurp from it.

The famous Granny-Wrestler reached the end of the rope and swung himself on board with his mighty arms. When he landed on the deck the whole boat seemed to shudder, as if it had been rammed by a whale. He cast a shadow over the other Vikings.

Ragnar was as tall as a fir tree. He had a beard that reached his ankles, and a sword so big that it could steer the ship. In fact he looked more like a bear dressed in clothes than a man.

Ragnar's voice boomed when he spoke.

"I am Ragnar, son of Hakon the Wolf-Hunter,

brother of Sven the Mace-Smasher. Even my mother had a name. She was Monika the Head-Basher-Inner."

There was a strong mumble of approval amongst the crew, but Ragnar was far from finished.

"I bully the meek, I spit on the weak, and I burp at the innocent. All before I even have my breakfast!" Applause started to break out. "I am a basher of peasants, an impaler of heads, a destroyer of cities and a scourge of nations!"

"HUZZAH!" the Vikings cried, jumping up and down. "Long live Ragnar the Granny-Wrestler!"

"And who are you lot?" he asked, when they finally stopped cheering.

Thorfinn's father stepped forward and proudly introduced himself and his crew.

"It's a fine honour to meet you! Please accept the hospitality of our ship," he said. "And, by the way, could we have your autograph?"

Ragnar the Granny-Wrestler laughed, and he pulled out his sword and cut an X into the side of the boat.

"There you go. You see, I cannot write, so that is my autograph. Now, where is my hospitality?"

Thorfinn's father was about to break open a barrel of their best ale, when Thorfinn appeared. He was carrying a tray of wooden cups filled with tea.

"Good day to you, my dear Mr Granny-Wrestler," he said, doffing his helmet with his free hand. "Would you care for a cup of tea?"

CHAPTER 9

All the Vikings on the ship stood in horrified silence. They were absolutely gobsmacked.

"A what?" said Ragnar. He looked down at Thorfinn like he was examining a small insect.

"Pinecone tea," said Thorfinn pleasantly. "As you can see, I've made enough for your men as well. It's very refreshing."

The famous Viking's face said everything. Ragnar the Granny-Wrestler looked as if he'd been slapped across the cheek with a large wet fish.

He glared at Thorfinn's father, who'd gone red, and then Erik the Ear-Masher, who'd gone white.

Suddenly, Ragnar pulled out his sword and swung it round his head.

"By Odin's trousers!" he roared. "Give me one good reason why I shouldn't throw this little twerp over the side!"

"Goodness me. Did I say something wrong?" said Thorfinn.

"Did you say something wrong?" said Chief Harald, trembling with shame. "Ragnar the Granny-Wrestler does not drink PINECONE TEA!"

The rest of the crew were just as embarrassed. They were furious that Thorfinn could shame them like this. In fact, some of them (especially Erik the

Ear-Masher and his son) agreed that he should be thrown over the side.

"Make him walk the plank!" they shouted. "This imbecile is no Viking! He's nothing but trouble! He's made us look like a bunch of idiots!"

"Thorfinn the Tea-Maker!" cried Olaf.

"I don't understand. You said to treat him like a very special guest," said Thorfinn to his father.

"Make Harald walk the plank too!" shouted Erik. "It's his fault for bringing Thorfinn!"

A few of the Vikings gasped. Once again, Erik the Ear-Masher had challenged their chief.

Thorfinn's father was having no more of this. He whipped out his sword, and Erik whipped out his. There was a mighty clash, and sparks flew everywhere. They locked their weapons together and came eye to eye, or rather, eyes to eye, as Erik only had the one.

"You rat!" cried Thorfinn's father.

"You dog!" Erik responded.

They duelled, splitting wood and ripping sails with every swipe and thrust. The crew gathered round, cheering, eager to see the action. Ragnar was thrilled to see such fine entertainment.

"Aha, now we're getting somewhere. A fight ... to the death!" he cried.

CHAPTER 10

Meanwhile, Thorfinn went and sat down nearby. He wasn't at all worried about his father, as he knew he was by far the best swordsman. He stretched a torn piece of sail across his knee, then he got a bit of charcoal and started to write.

Thorfinn was right, as it turned out. Erik was no match for Harald. They didn't call him the Skull-Splitter for nothing.

With an almighty **CRACK!** Harald split Erik's sword in two. Everyone applauded. Even Ragnar was impressed.

Erik stared down at its shattered remains. "That was my fifth favourite sword!" he snarled, then tossed the hilt over the side and charged at Harald.

Thorfinn's father didn't flinch, didn't move a muscle, until Erik was just feet away. He thrust his right arm out in front of him, his fist pointing straight at Erik's face.

THWOCK!

Erik rebounded, his one eye rolling, his cheeks wobbling like jelly, and fell against the mast.

Harold joked, "You've got five swords. It's a pity you don't have any more heads." This brought gales of laughter from the crew.

Erik staggered about holding his head, crying, "THE BELLS! THE BELLS! THEY WON'T STOP." The crew were bent double now. Erik steeled himself, roared like a bear and charged at Harald once again.

Just then, Thorfinn handed the famous Viking a bit of cloth he'd been writing on.

Everyone froze, even Thorfinn's father and Erik, who were by now sprawled across the deck wrestling cheek to cheek. They half expected to see Thorfinn being chucked over the side of the boat.

"You again? What's this?" said Ragnar. He opened out the cloth. It said:

"It's your name," said Thorfinn. "That's how you write it down. I can teach you if you like. It would probably make your fans a lot happier when you sign autographs."

For one moment, Ragnar looked at the cloth, then at Thorfinn. Then he looked at the cloth again. Nobody was sure how he was going to react.

Then a booming laugh erupted from his chest. He ruffled Thorfinn's hair, picked him up, danced about with him, and then put him down again.

"The boy can teach me to write!" he exclaimed. "Ha! Think on it. Next time I meet the King, he will be *sooo* impressed."

The entire crew sighed with relief.

After he'd learned to write his own name, Ragnar
the Granny-Wrestler left the boat and hauled his
way across the divide between the two ships.

"Set a course for the royal capital!" he roared to
his men.

When he got to his own longship he heaved
himself on board and stood erect on the deck. He
turned, and waved at them with his sword.

"Bye, Thorfinn. When I see the King I will sign my
autograph for him, like this."

He held up the cloth.

They sailed off before Thorfinn could get Ragnar
to turn it the right way up.

"Well," said his father as they watched Ragnar's
ship disappear towards Norway. "It looks like we've
found another use for you, young Thorfinn."

"What do you mean?" said Erik. "Because of him,
everyone will think we're a bunch of twits."

"Because of him, you overgrown jellyfish," said

Oswald, leaning on his cane, "we are a friend of Ragnar. The King himself may hear of us."

"Thorfinn the Pencil-Sharpener?" said Olaf, but this time only his own father responded. Nobody else laughed.

"Ha!" snorted Erik, and he stomped off, muttering about revenge.

CHAPTER 11

The sun went down, and they sailed on towards the west. When the sun came up again, Thorfinn still couldn't see Scotland. In fact, he saw nothing at all but the swelling sea in each direction. And so on the next day, and the next day. In fact, Thorfinn was beginning to lose track of time. Although he'd read about it many times, he'd never imagined that the world was this big.

And then, one morning, as the bright red sun was rising in the east, Thorfinn woke up and rubbed his eyes. He got up and looked over the side.

He saw land.

"At last!" he said aloud. "We're here."

"That's right," said Oswald, who'd been up for a while to brew the tea. "Scotland."

The shore was too rocky to land, and so they sailed down the coast, looking for a bay or a beach. They passed a small boat with two boys fishing over the side. Thorfinn gave them a friendly wave.

"Don't wave at the Scots, fool!" Olaf smacked his hand away. His hawk was perched on his arm, and he stroked the bird's head. "We're here to pillage and destroy, not to make friends with them."

Thorfinn shrugged. He couldn't understand such rudeness. The boys were waving back anyway, so he just ignored Olaf and carried on waving. Then, whistling happily, he went over and fed Percy, whose cage hung off the mast.

"Why do you keep that mangy pigeon?" said Olaf, looking at the bird with disgust.

"It's a very useful bird, the pigeon," replied Thorfinn.

Olaf snorted.

"Ha! Useful?" he said. "Can it hunt? Can it kill? No. It is useless."

Thorfinn paid no heed to this. He took Percy out and started stroking his speckly feathers.

"Tell you what. Let's have a bet," Olaf said.

"What do you mean?" asked Thorfinn.

"Your mangy pigeon against my magnificent hawk," said Olaf. "Let's set them off. Let's see how useful your pigeon really is. Let's see what it comes back with, if it comes back at all. Maybe my hawk will eat it."

The deck echoed with laughter, as men gathered round to watch.

Olaf took the hood off the hawk. It had sharp, ruthless eyes and a deadly beak. It took a quick look around. Then Olaf raised his arm

and it flew away.

Everyone watched as the hawk flew round the

boat in a circle. The circles got wider and wider as it scanned the sea for prey.

"It's hunting for fish," said Olaf.

Thorfinn watched as the hawk began hovering over an area of sea.

"See," said Olaf. "It's discovered a shoal of fish below the surface."

Thorfinn turned away and wrote a message down on a slip of cloth. He tied it to Percy's leg and set the pigeon off.

Percy flew to the north, the direction they'd just come from.

"Ha! Look at this – Thorfinn the Pigeon-Fancier!" said Olaf. This brought another big laugh from the crew.

After a few minutes of circling, Olaf's hawk

swooped down to the water and sank its claws underneath. In a frantic splash, the bird emerged with a small fish, and brought it back to the ship.

As it dropped the fish into Olaf's hand, the crew clapped and cheered. This was a great feat for a Viking boy.

Thorfinn clapped too. It was only a small fish, but hawks were very difficult to train, and it couldn't have been easy for Olaf to do.

"Olaf the Hawk-Master!" cried one of the other Vikings. This brought another cheer. Erik the Ear-Masher came up and congratulated his son by slapping him on the shoulders.

"Ha! I am very proud, son. You've shown you can handle a hawk, so how do you like the name Hawk-Master?"

"I like it, Father," he said. "But I'd prefer Olaf the Dimwit-Whacker, for when I've whacked this dimwit here."

"You have yet to win the bet, so do not celebrate," said Harald. "Let's see what my son's bird brings back."

"Indeed," said Thorfinn. "In fact, it shouldn't be much longer now."

The whole crew watched the sky.

CHAPTER 12

Sure enough, after just a few more minutes, Percy returned and landed on Thorfinn's shoulder. Thorfinn removed the slip of cloth from the bird's leg and unrolled it.

"Ah, good news," he said. "They replied."

Thorfinn read what was written on the cloth.

"Oh dear." He walked up to the back of the ship straight away to speak to the man at the rudder. The rest of the crew followed, puzzled.

"Who replied?" they said. "And what do you mean, 'Oh dear'?"

"Why, the boys in the fishing boat, of course," Thorfinn said.

While the rest of the crew looked at each other, bemused, Thorfinn turned to the man at the rudder. He pointed at the headland rising up in front of them.

"Pardon me, helmsman, but please take a big turn left here. We're about to sail into some rocks. They're just underneath the water, right in front of the headland."

Quickly, the helmsman steered the ship in a wide circle round the headland. As they passed, everyone aboard could see the rocks just under the surface. They would be a death trap to any ship.

"By Thor's teeth!" said Thorfinn's father. "I do believe you've saved the ship."

There was a gasp of astonishment among the crew. No one could work out how Thorfinn knew the rocks were ahead of them.

"It's easy," said Thorfinn. "I sent a message to the boys in the boat. I know their language, after all. I told them to follow the hawk, because he'd found that big shoal of fish. In return, they gave me directions."

Everyone turned to see a small boat sailing towards the shoal of fish. Thorfinn waved at them again, and the boys on the boat waved back.

Erik the Ear-Masher and his son were amazed.
Olaf looked down at the tiny fish his own bird had
caught.

Oswald banged his stick on the deck and stood up.

"Now who's laughing, idiots! Thorfinn the Navigator! Thorfinn the Ship-Master!"

The whole crew was confused now. They didn't know what to do. Thorfinn had saved their ship, but they couldn't possibly cheer someone like him. Instead, they looked down at their feet like a bunch of schoolboys, and mumbled their thanks under their breath.

Thorfinn's father came up to him, scratching his head.

"I can't work it out," he said. " How did we manage to raise a boy like you?"

But Thorfinn's toughest test was about to come.

On the other side of the headland they found a sheltered bay where they could moor the ship and go ashore. They could see a quiet Scottish village nearby, nestled in the hills. Nothing lay between it and the crew of bloodthirsty Viking warriors.

CHAPTER 13

Once they'd anchored the ship, Thorfinn's father had all the shields taken out of the store and put in a big pile on the deck. The Vikings formed a line to receive their shield from their chief. This was a tradition among them. It was the only time Vikings were ever known to queue.

After each man got his shield, he jumped off the side of the boat, landed in the water and waded ashore. Oswald was lowered down on a rope, yelling all the way.

"Watch it! You shower of elks!"

"Shut up, you old relic!" they replied.

Finally, the whole crew assembled on the beach, and they started to march inland. Oswald had to be carried all the way.

They marched over some hills and through a very thick forest, until finally they reached the edge of the woods. There, hidden by the trees, they watched the peaceful village they'd seen from the boat.

The village had a church, an inn and a market place, and it

was surrounded by fields of golden wheat. Smoke rose from chimneys, and children played with their dogs in the street.

"Hmm, what a quaint village," said Thorfinn. "Pardon me, my dear sirs, but isn't it a shame to burn it to the ground?"

There was a snort of outrage. The other Vikings looked like they wanted to burn him along with the village.

"Once and for all, let us rid ourselves of this young upstart!" cried Erik. "How can we get worked up into our Viking wrath with this peace-loving fool behind us crying out, 'No, don't burn that!' and 'Oh, don't loot this!'? It's very off-putting, you know. He has all the fighting spirit of a plate of boiled turnips!"

The other Vikings started chattering their agreement. "It's embarrassing! We're professionals, you know!"

"Bah! I'll have none of this!" cried Thorfinn's father. He swung his sword and smashed it into a tree. Splinters flew everywhere. "He won't be behind us, Ear-Masher, he'll be in front of us."

Erik screwed up his face, puzzled.

"Eh?"

Thorfinn's father leaned down and took Thorfinn's shoulder. "Now then, young Thorfinn, I have a job for you. You must not fail us. Do you understand?"

"Yes, Father," he replied.

"You speak their language, so you will go down

to the village and deliver our terms. This is the message: 'Give us everything you have or we destroy the village.' Do you understand?"

Thorfinn stroked his chin. "Mmm ... then what?" he said.

"Oh, it doesn't matter," replied his father. "We'll probably destroy the village anyway. But sometimes they run away with all the loot before we get a chance to nick it. This way, perhaps they'll give us all their loot first. You see?"

The other Vikings agreed that this was a very good idea.

"And what if they say no?" Thorfinn asked.

"Run for it," said his father. "That's why we're sending you and not Oswald. He's too old, and can't run as fast. In fact, he can't run at all."

Before Thorfinn had a chance to ask any more questions, his father slapped him on the back and pushed him through the trees towards the village.

"Go on, quickly!" he bellowed.

Thorfinn stumbled off in the direction of the village, while the Viking raiders waited under cover of the trees.

The last they saw of Thorfinn, just before he disappeared out of sight, he was walking up the main street. He took his helmet off to a passing old lady, before declaring loudly, "Good day, dear madam! And what a beautiful afternoon."

CHAPTER 14

The afternoon wore on, and the sun crept across
the sky. There was still no sign of Thorfinn. The
Vikings were getting very bored and frustrated.
They were sitting around on the ground, or propped
up against trees. Their weapons were sheathed in
their belts, and some men even fell asleep.

"Where in the name of Thor can that boy be?"
said Erik.

"Perhaps he's still discussing terms," said
Thorfinn's father.

But there was no sign of panic or alarm in the

village. The chimneys were still smoking. The children were still playing with their dogs in the street. It didn't look like a village that knew it was about to be invaded by a Viking horde.

"I bet you he's playing bowls with them or something," said Olaf.

"Yeah, or maybe he's offered to do their dishes," said Erik.

The restless Vikings started to stir.

"Perhaps he's forgotten all about delivering terms and gone off to pick flowers!"

"What are we waiting for?" said Olaf. "Let's attack!"

There was a chorus of agreement amongst the Vikings. They all picked up their swords and shields.

"Wait," said Oswald. "Give Thorfinn a chance, you baboons!"

"That fool! No!" came the reply. "It's time to attack! Let's go! Yes!"

Just as the whole mob was about to break its cover and hurtle down the hill, someone caught sight of a figure coming towards them.

"It's Thorfinn!" said Harald. "At last!"

And he was right. It was Thorfinn. He was carrying what looked like a big basket covered with a cloth. From a distance, it looked like it was piled high with stuff – valuables, perhaps.

"Am I seeing right?" said Erik. "Is that tray filled with goodies, or what?"

As Thorfinn got nearer and nearer, taking great

care carrying the basket, some of the Vikings started slapping each other on the back, and even discussing gold prices. It looked like Thorfinn had finally come up with the goods.

At last, Thorfinn pushed through the trees. He had a huge smile on his face as he stopped in front of them all and put down the basket.

And what was the precious cargo he was carrying?

He whipped away the cloth.

Scones.

What else?

With lots of jam and cream. They were still piping hot. They had just been baked.

The whole crew stared, horrified, as if they'd just

found out that great Thor himself had a part-time
job as a dung collector.

"Care for a scone, anyone?" Thorfinn said happily.

"Bah! What is the meaning of this?" cried his
father. "You were supposed to come back with the
loot!"

"Oh, the loot, yes," said Thorfinn. Before he could
go on, Erik cut in.

"You've brought us back scones!" he said. "Did we ask for scones? We are fearsome Viking warriors! We're only happy when we're hacking and impaling and wreaking havoc. We only eat meat. We don't eat scones! We've never eaten scones! We hate scones! Scones are for idiots! Death to all scone-makers!"

"Ah, but they're not any old scones," said Thorfinn. "We've got jam and cream and everything. Mrs Ross, the blacksmith's wife, baked them for me. Try them. They're the best scones I've ever eaten."

Now the Vikings were outraged. They wanted to tie Thorfinn to a tree and pelt him with his precious scones.

CHAPTER 15

"That's enough!" they cried. "Let's get this numbskull once and for all! He's an embarrassment! He is no Viking!"

Thorfinn's father managed to bring some calm to the scene by swiping his axe at a tree, cutting it in half and sending it crashing to the ground. He stood between the other Vikings and his son. His eye started twitching again, and he leaned down and addressed Thorfinn sternly.

"Bah! Now, look here. Did you or did you not deliver our terms to the village?"

"I didn't," Thorfinn replied innocently, which made the Vikings erupt in fury again. Some of them drew their swords, intent on running him through. Even Thorfinn's father looked like he had given up with his wayward son. He turned away, disappointed, and shook his head.

"Well," continued Thorfinn. "I didn't think it would be very wise. Not with that massive army camped on the hill over there."

It took a moment for this to sink in. The men started shouting with anger again, but then they stopped. Thorfinn's father turned back to look at his son. Meanwhile, Thorfinn sat down and picked up a steaming hot scone.

"What? What do you mean?" said Harald.

Thorfinn bit into the scone with relish. He didn't think it was polite to speak with his mouth full, so he waited until he had finished before he replied.

By that time his fellow Vikings were just about pulling their hair out with suspense.

"Come, I'll show you," he said.

He got up, taking his scone with him, and led them up to the brow of the hill. From there they could see all around. He pointed out a hill on the other side of the village.

"There," he said.

Sure enough, they saw campfires, banners fluttering in the breeze, weapons propped up in pyramids, and men clad in leather armour riding warhorses. An entire army was camped there.

They couldn't believe it. Right under their noses. And nobody had noticed.

Just then, it struck them. If they'd attacked the

village, they would have been wiped out. All Vikings liked a good battle, but fighting against an entire army was asking a bit much ... even for them.

"Well, when I got to the village they did get a bit of a shock," Thorfinn continued. "You see, I am dressed like a Viking, so they thought I wanted to hurt them. Indeed, they were about to send a messenger to fetch the army. But when they saw my manners they decided that it was impossible for me to be a Viking. I was far too nice. So they invited me to stay for afternoon tea instead. They are terribly polite people, these Scots."

"Afternoon tea?" said Erik, horrified, like it was some form of torture.

"By the hounds of hell!" said Harald. "Do you realise that it is only because of Thorfinn that we are still alive? If we'd sent someone else down there, and if we'd attacked the village, then we'd all have been slaughtered."

They were completely stunned, but didn't have a moment to lose. They had to get back to the ship before they were discovered.

There was no doubt about it. Thorfinn had saved them all. Again.

CHAPTER 16

The Vikings marched to the ship and set sail right away. They were leaving Scotland empty-handed, and without ruining any villages. Being Vikings, they were a bit disappointed about that, but it could have been a lot worse. They might never have left at all if it hadn't been for Thorfinn.

Now, the cheers and the songs were all for him. It felt like Thorfinn had won them a great victory.

"Long live Thorfinn! Thorfinn has saved us! Go on, then, I WILL have a scone!"

They sailed east, towards home, as the red sun

set behind them. Thorfinn's father broke out the ale, and they hoisted Thorfinn up on their shoulders and carried him around the ship in triumph.

Now they decided that being nice might not be such a bad thing after all. They stood around swapping polite remarks. They even started saying "Pardon me" after they belched.

All, that is, except for Olaf and his father Erik. They stood alone at the prow of the ship, folding their arms and grumbling.

"Good day, indeed!" scoffed Erik. "Anyone saying 'good day' to me better watch. They'll get an axe through their head."

"Just wait. We'll get our revenge, Father," said Olaf.

"Yes, we will."

And they swore on it.

It was Harald who brought a hush to proceedings. This time he didn't use his axe to shut everyone up. Instead he picked his son up in a big bear hug. Thorfinn couldn't understand what all the fuss was about.

"You are a very nice young Viking," said Thorfinn's father.

"Thank you, dear Father. How very nice of you to say so," Thorfinn replied.

"He is," added Oswald, laughing. "Very very nice indeed!"

A booming laugh came from Harald's chest. "Why, that's it!" he said. "You have it, Oswald. My son has won his name. From this day forward let Thorfinn the Very-Very-Nice-Indeed be a Viking hero. Let legends be written about him!"

The crew cheered. "Thorfinn the Very-Very-Nice-Indeed! Let tales be told about him. Let songs be sung about him."

"HUZZAH!" came the reply.

"Let his deeds be told in stories round campfires for generations to come!"

"HUZZAH!" they replied again.

And they finished all the scones.

RICHARD THE
PICTURE-CONQUEROR

DAVID THE
STORY-CHIEF

DAVID MACPHAIL left home at eighteen to travel the world and have adventures. After working as a chicken wrangler, a ghost-tour guide and a waiter on a tropical island, he now has the sensible job of writing about yetis and Vikings. At home in Perthshire, Scotland, he exists on a diet of cream buns and zombie movies.

RICHARD MORGAN was born and raised by goblins on the Yorkshire moors. After running away to New Zealand to play with yachts and paint backgrounds for Disney TV he returned to the UK to write and illustrate children's books. He now lives in Cambridge, England, and has a family of goblins of his own.

VIKING NAME GENERATOR

Follow these simple steps to find your Viking name!

1. What's the *first letter* of your *first name*?
Your Viking *first name* begins with the same letter.

BOYS

Alrick	Norgrid
Bjorn	Olaf
Cnut	Parek
Dagfin	Queeg
Einar	Ragnar
Fiske	Sven
Gart	Thorfast
Harek	Ulf
Ingmar	Viggo
Jari	Welk
Kare	Xander
Leif	Yanulf
Magnus	Zarek

GIRLS

Astrid	Nari
Brenna	Olthilda
Correy	Poyda
Dagny	Qwin
Erika	Ragnilda
Freya	Sylvie
Gerda	Thora
Hilda	Una
Ingrid	Vynhilda
Jorunn	Werda
Kari	Xansa
Lara	Yiva
Mara	Zara

2. What *month* were you born? Use that to find the *first half* of your Viking *surname*.
Pick from three options.

JANUARY	Monk Ox Tongue	**JULY**	Bishop Bottom Shield
FEBRUARY	Head Squid Tonsil	**AUGUST**	Finger Hound Pinkie
MARCH	Bear Peasant Raven	**SEPTEMBER**	Appendix Hawk Monkey
APRIL	Big Toe Little Toe Kraken	**OCTOBER**	Elk King Spear
MAY	Arm Ear Skull	**NOVEMBER**	Granny Lord Wolf
JUNE	Bone Brain Nose	**DECEMBER**	Hammer Knight Sword

Turn over to find out the second half of your Viking surname!

3. What *day* of the month were you born? Use that to find the *second half* of your Viking *surname.*

1 – Catapulter	17 – Impaler
2 – Mangler	18 – Eater
3 – Wrangler	19 – Breaker
4 – Splitter	20 – Crusher
5 – Lopper-offer	21 – Smasher
6 – Slinger	22 – Hammerer
7 – Biffer	23 – Basher
8 – Thumper	24 – Squasher
9 – Skewerer	25 – Mincer
10 – Slayer	26 – Grinder
11 – Wrestler	27 – Squisher
12 – Stapler	28 – Farter
13 – Stamper	29 – Shish-kebbaber
14 – Wrencher	30 – Stretcher
15 – Biter	31 – Chucker
16 – Throttler	

FOR EXAMPLE

David MacPhail was born on 22nd May,[*] so his Viking name is:

DAGFIN THE SKULL-HAMMERER

What's your Viking name? What about your friends?

[*]Please send cards and pressies to 76 Hackenbush, Indgar Village, Norway

VIKING JOKES!

Why do Vikings struggle to learn the alphabet?
Because they spend so long at C.

Where do Viking schoolchildren get sent when they have stomach pain?
To the school Norse.

How did the Viking feel after rowing across the North Sea?
He was Thor all over.

Why did the Viking cross the road?
He was eating the chicken.

How do Vikings send secret messages?
By Norse code.

PERCY THE PIGEON HAS BROUGHT
THORFINN A SECRET MESSAGE.
CAN YOU DECODE IT TO SAVE THE DAY?

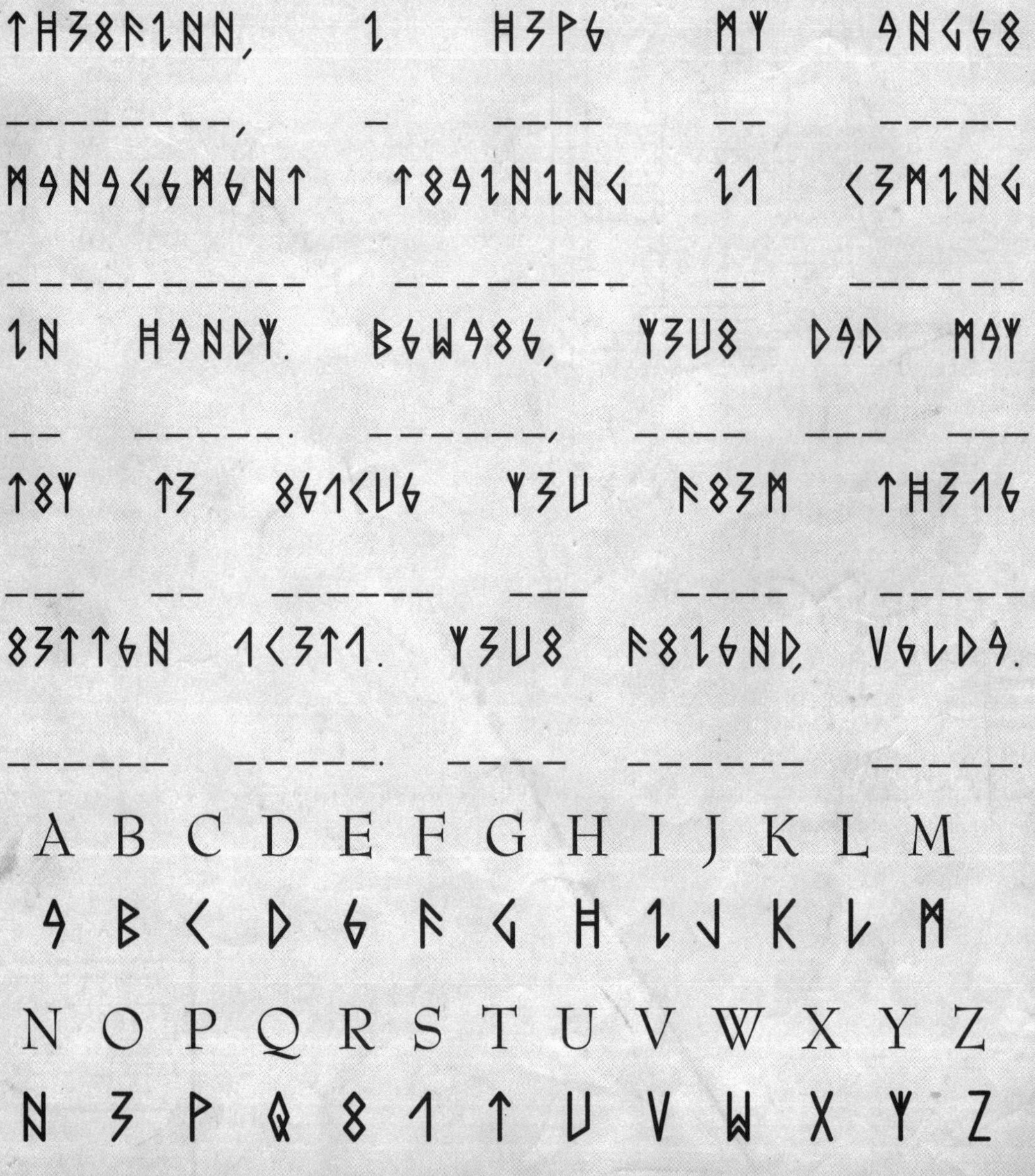

_____, _ ____ __ _____

_____ _____ __ _____

__ _____. _____, ____ ___ ___

___ __ _____ ___ ____ _____

_____ _____. ____ _____, _____.

A	B	C	D	E	F	G	H	I	J	K	L	M

N	O	P	Q	R	S	T	U	V	W	X	Y	Z

VICIOUS VIKING POCKET PHRASES

Hello
Hallo!

Please
RAAAAAR! (Vikings have no word for please. Shouting "RAAAR!" at the top of your voice is as close as you'll get.)

Thanks
Again, RAAARR! (Vikings don't say thanks either.)

Can I please have...
Kan jeg RAAAAAR vennglist fa...

   ...your gold?
   ...gull?

   ...your treasure
   ...dine verdisaker?

What time does the longship depart?
Nar gar langskip vike?

I'm sorry, I'm allergic to...
Jeg beklager et heg er allergisk mot...

   ...all fruit and vegetables
   ...all frukt og gronnsaker

   ...tea
   ...te

   ...visitors
   ...besokende

   ...soap
   ...såpe

Please help! I've just eaten a vegetable!
RAAAAAR behage hjelpe! Jeg har akkurat spist en gronnsak!

I'd like to send a message by carrier pigeon.
Jeg vil gjerne sende en melding ved hjelp av brevduer.

Where's the loot, toadface?
Hvor er tyvegods padde ansiktet?

PERCY THE PIGEON POST

EST. 799AD   THORSDAY 23RD JUNE   PRICE: ONE EARLOB

SKULL-SPLITTING NEWS

In what will forever be known as the **Awful Invasion** the Scots have narrowly missed being invaded by a band of marauding Vikings, led by the fearsome Chief of Indgar, Harald the Skull-Splitter. "His son, Thorfinn the Very-Very-Nice-Indeed, is his only weak spot," confided an anonymous source with disturbing ears.

SPORTING HEADLINES

It is the weekend of the annual **Gruesome Games.** Word on the beach is that Thorfinn the Very-Very-Nice-Indeed, wise-man Oswald and (hold on to your axes), Velda – a GIRL – must save their village from the clutches of Magnus the Bone-Breaker. Odds are on for a new Chief of Indgar by Monday.

TORTUROUS TRAVEL

If you happen to be kidnapped by the **Rotten Scots** and held at Castle Red Wolf, you'll find plenty of activities for friendly non-Vikings, such as sewing and fishing. All under the careful instruction of its most famous captive, Thorfinn the Very-Very-Nice-Indeed. Early booking essential for he may be 'rescued' at any moment.

FOULSOME FOOD

It's all about Le Poisson (that's FISH to you boneheads). The King of Norway is on his way to Indgar and he expects a most **Disgusting Feast.** Can Thorfinn the Very-Very-Nice-Indeed organise a banquet of beasts? With a poisoner at large? The heat is on in the kitchen...

Collect all of Thorfinn's adventures!

Keep reading for a sneak peak of

THORFINN THE NICEST VIKING

and the Gruesome Games

CHAPTER 1

Indgar was like any normal Viking village, with sword fighting in the morning, wrestling in the afternoon, and at least three big punch-ups before dinner. And that was just for the old folk.

Around lunchtime the women of the village gathered round the well with their laundry. Not that they ever did any laundry. Usually they just catapulted it into the fjord. It would almost always wash up on shore the next day, slightly cleaner than it had been when it went in.

One of the women spotted the chief's son – a boy called Thorfinn – stepping out from behind a large sheet covering the great hall.

"What are you up to, Thorfinn?" she asked.

"Good day, dear ladies," said Thorfinn, removing his helmet. "You'll be the first to see my new surprise. Ta da!" He pulled the sheet away.

The women's screams could be heard on the other side of the village.

Thorfinn's father, Harald the Skull-Splitter, Chief of Indgar, sat alone in his chamber, wrapped in furs. He was writing down a list of the village's competitors for this year's International Gruesome Games.
It did not make good reading. The only contest they had a chance of winning was belching.

Harald scratched his head and looked around

his private chamber. The walls were adorned with stags' heads, trophies and souvenirs from his many adventures. Harald eyed the village's ceremonial sword, Whirlwind. He had carried it into battle many times. It was a symbol of his power as village chief.

His eyes moved slowly to the empty space next to it, where his ceremonial shield, Sword-Blunter, used to sit. Whirlwind and Sword-Blunter belonged together, but the shield had been lost in battle many years ago. The chief of the neighbouring village,

Magnus the Bone-Breaker, had it now.

Magnus would be at the games too, thought Harald. He would be gloating over the shield and showing it off to everyone. Harald would do anything to get it back.

Suddenly, half the men of the village stormed into his house, yelling over each other and trying to get through his chamber door.

"CHIEF!" "BOSS!"

Their faces pressed together as they all became stuck, their eyes bulging out of their heads, their arms sticking out all over the place.

"EEK!"

"HUUYYYYY! BOSS, LISTEN!"

"BLEUUUUGH! CHIEF, QUICK!"

Harald did not like to be interrupted. He rose from his seat, glaring at the men with venom. Harald was famous for his incredibly twitchy eye. It could strike fear into the heart of anyone, even the fiercest of the fierce. And it was quite useful at times like this.

He deployed the twitch. The men froze in the doorway, terrified.

"WHAT is the meaning of this?" Harald roared. "Barging into my house, my own private chamber. Well, what do you have to say for yourselves, you fish-faced idiots?"

For a moment nobody spoke. Lots of eyes just looked round at one another. Then, it was as if a spring had been released, as the men exploded through the door and fell in a heap at Harald's feet.

"S-s-sorry, Chief," said one of them sheepishly. "B-b-but it's your son, Thorfinn."

"He's gone too far this time," said another.

"You've got to stop him," said one more.

Harald sank into his throne, his head in his hands.

"Ugh!" he sighed. "What has that boy of mine been up to now?"